SUMMER BREAK

D1313272

Mike Doyle

Fulton Books, Inc.
Meadville, PA

Published by Fulton Books 2021

ISBN 978-1-64952-515-4 (paperback)
ISBN 978-1-63710-149-0 (hardcover)
ISBN 978-1-64952-516-1 (digital)

Printed in the United States of America

Special thanks to my wife, Cindy, for her support and inspiration during the writing of this book.

1

S pring had arrived, and summer break was less than a month away. The last few days of school seemed to go on for eternity. Every second seemed like a minute, every minute an hour, and every hour a day. For two thirteen-year-old boys, nothing was as exciting as the end of the school year, except maybe Christmas or the county fair. It was a longing for those open spaces, an infatuation you might say. Luke and Josh had been looking forward to going fishing, swimming, camping out, staying up late, and a whole bunch of other activities, especially going to Logan Lake. That's where the girls from school hung out. All the boys liked to go there, take their shirts off, and walk around to try and impress the girls. Not that any of them had any muscles or anything. Heck, all that was ever heard was gigglin' when these Mr. America wannabes walked by. But it was still fun. And for some strange reason, the girls sure did look a lot prettier this year. It was the darndest thing.

"Luke! LUCAS MEYERS!"

"Huh? Oh, yes, Mrs. Cargood?"

"Do you mind explaining to the class what you are doing?"

"I-I was just looking out the window."

"Well, looking out the window is not going to help you pass this class, young man. Now pay attention."

"Y-yes ma'am."

Darn that Mrs. Cargood, thought Luke. She was the meanest teacher there ever was. *How on earth did "good" get put into her last name? She's the farthest thing from that. Oh well, only two more weeks of her class, and she would just be a memory. A bad one at that.*

The school bell rang. It couldn't have come at a better time. Luke and Josh were ready to go. It was about a fifteen-minute ride home for Luke and ten minutes for Josh. Both boys lived outside of town, but they didn't mind the ride. There was always something in the ditch alongside the road to look for. Anything from discarded soda bottles that could be turned in at the store for two cents each to an old tire that could be salvaged for a tree swing.

The two boys normally hung around the playground for a few minutes after school to let the traffic clear, but for today Luke had to get right home. With the warm weather came additional chores. Not ones that he was particularly fond of, but if it helped his dad, he didn't really complain. Henry, Luke's dad, had been injured a couple of years earlier, so Luke carried more responsibility around the house than most boys his age.

"Lucas, is that you?" his mother yelled as the screen door slammed shut.

"Yes, ma'am!" Luke shouted. "Just getting home from school."

He knew that when she called him Lucas, she had something on her mind. And when his mom spoke, he listened. Luke also knew when chores were finished, there was usually some kind of treat.

What could it be today? Luke thought. *An apple pie or maybe chocolate brownies, or possibly one of her famous malts.* It didn't matter. Whatever it was, Luke knew it would be delicious. His mother was the best cook he knew. Probably in the whole world, he thought. It sure did make doing chores a lot easier when there was some incentive to get finished.

"Better get your chores done. We got some things to do after dinner," said his mother.

"Yes, ma'am," said Luke.

"Your father needs some help at the barn."

"On my way."

Sarah Meyers was a very disciplined, high-moral, common-sense woman. Growing up in poverty, she knew how to get by on very little. After Henry's accident, much of the burden of taking care of the family fell upon her shoulders, but she was not discouraged. She labored day and night to ensure that family needs were taken care of. Never a Sunday went by that she did not attend church. It seemed to be her motivation. She knew things would work out for them.

Pausing to see what treat his mom had made, he noticed his mom giving him the eye.

"Don't worry, young man. There'll be something here for you when you're finished." Luke smiled from ear to ear and headed for the barn.

Luke looked around until he found his dad. He stood there for a few seconds watching him work, realizing just how lucky he was to have a dad that took the time to teach him things that most boys his age would not know until they were grown, if at all. He considered himself fortunate to have a dad he could also say was one of his best friends.

Henry Meyers was a wholesome, keen-minded, simple man. Until the day he was injured on the job, he was a hard worker who didn't mind lending a helping hand to anyone. An injury had left him completely blind in one eye and limited use of his left arm. Work was hard to find. A few odd jobs, a garden, and a monthly check from the government kept food on the table. Staying busy helped him to not think about what could have been. All in all, he had much to be thankful for—a home that was paid for, a good son, and a loving wife. He really didn't need anything else.

"Hey, Dad!" Luke shouted.

"Hey, son. How was school today?"

"Oh, it was okay, I guess," stammered Luke.

"Hmm," said Henry. "Sounds like you have something on your mind."

"Well, it's just that Mrs. Cargood is so rude. She doesn't give us any slack. Always hollerin', or t—"

Henry cut him off. "Whoa, young man. Being a teacher is no easy job. It takes a special person to deal with that many kids all day long. And there's probably some other things that you don't know about her. You see, she lost a son to a disease when he was younger than you. She had a very hard time with it. After a while, she and her husband divorced. I don't think he understood how much she missed her son. A lot has happened to that woman. She's just probably still bitter about losing her family. I think if you show her a little respect and compassion, you'd be amazed how much she would appreciate it. So put that in your memory box."

"Mmm, okay," Luke quietly said. He knew anytime his dad said "memory box," it was something important and he needed to remember it.

Luke stood there like a mannequin in a store window until his subconscious awoke. *I wonder where Mrs. Cargood's son is buried? Should I go see for myself?* he thought. "No," said Luke, not realizing he had answered out loud.

"What's that, son?" his dad questioned.

Luke snapped out of his trance. "Nothin', Dad."

"Let's get done with these chores, son. Hand me that wrench on the table and make sure all the animals are fed. Your mom just about has supper ready."

"Great," said Luke.

That evening after supper, Luke's mother asked him if he had thought about getting Mrs. Cargood a gift for the end of the school year.

"A gift? Heck, what for?"

"Now, Luke, it's appropriate to buy a gift for your teacher at the end of the year. It shows how much you appreciate her dedication and hard work throughout the school year."

Sarah thought for a minute and decided on a gift he couldn't go wrong with.

"How 'bout a paperweight, Luke?" she said.

"A paper what?" asked Luke.

"Oh, Luke, a paperweight. You know, when the teacher gets her papers in order, she puts it on top of them to keep them from getting shuffled around. It also adds some nice decor to her desk."

"Yeah, I guess that would be okay. I think that's what she uses her stapler for, though," said Luke.

"Then its settled. When we get the dishes done, we can go to the department store and see what they have. I don't think they close till eight. That okay with you, son?"

"Sure, mom. That sounds great." Anyway, that would give him a chance to look for some fishing supplies he would need for the summer.

When they arrived at Henley's Department Store, Luke went one way and his mom the other. Luke headed straight for the sporting goods. There was all kinds of neat fishing gadgets, and Luke had been saving his allowance just for the occasion.

Two men came walking down the aisle while Luke had his face buried in the lures. The men were talking to each other and didn't even see him. Luke raised up and took a step back to get a better look at the entire display. One of the men ran into him and nearly knocked him down. They looked at each other and the man said, "Watch it, kid." Luke felt like saying, "You watch where you're going," but he knew better. His dad told him long ago that when someone is rude or inconsiderate, just smile at them.

And this he did! When the man saw Luke smiling, he had a puzzled look on his face. He turned to the other man and mumbled something then looked over his shoulder again at Luke, still with the same puzzled look. Luke kept smiling until the two men and the shovels they were carrying turned the corner and were out of sight.

"Geez, I wonder what their problem is?" Luke said to himself. "Oh well, let's see. Where was I?"

Sarah shopped around for a while and then spotted what she was looking for—the "perfect" paperweight. It was getting late and time to head home. Now came the hard part—finding Luke. A boy his age could be anywhere in the store. Her instinct served her right, though. The sporting goods.

"Luke! Come see, son. Mrs. Cargood should like this present," she said in an anxious tone.

Luke studied it closely, then his eyes widened. "But, Mom, I can't give her anything that says Number One Teacher. She knows what everyone thinks about her," Luke said stubbornly.

"Lucas Meyers, I didn't raise you to talk bad about people behind their backs. She gives her time every day to help prepare you kids for the future. The least you can do is show a little appreciation," his mother snapped.

Luke remembered what his dad said about the "memory box." He thought for a second, looked at his mom, and politely said, "You're right, I don't know what I was thinking." As Luke finished gathering his fishing tackle, his mom shook her head and thought to herself, *Sometimes I just don't know which side of the road that boy is on.*

Anyway, Luke had a plan. He would give Mrs. Cargood her gift on the last day of school, after the final bell had rang, and all the kids had left. That way, no one would ever know except him and the teacher. Well, the final day of school came, and then the final bell. As the class emptied, Luke slowly walked up to Mrs. Cargood's desk. It seemed like it took forever. He stood there and didn't say a word. After a few seconds, Mrs. Cargood looked up with a puzzled look on her face.

"Is there something I can help you with, Luke?" she said.

"Well, I just wanted to give you this," Luke said hesitantly.

Mrs. Cargood looked down at his trembling hands as he produced a small wrapped box with a smashed bow. She sat there staring for eternity, or so it seemed. Then she looked up into his eyes.

"Sorry about the bow. It kinda got messed up in my backpack," said Luke.

All of a sudden, without any warning, a tear rolled down her face. Luke didn't know what to think. She just kept staring at him. Luke looked around the room to make sure he knew where the door was 'cause she didn't look so happy. Just as he was getting ready to turn and run, she grabbed him. Lord, he didn't know what to do. She was squeezing him so hard that he couldn't scream. Finally, she released her death grip on him and managed to open her present. She took one look at it and started bawling all over again. Luke swallowed hard, not knowing what to expect next. Then she muttered, "Oh Luke, this is the nicest present anyone has ever given me." Boy, was he relieved that she was happy. Then, suddenly, she grabbed his face and gave him a kiss right on the cheek. He stood there in shock for a minute. After regaining his composure, he knew that kiss was one secret that no one would ever find out about.

I guess Mom and Dad were right about her, thought Luke.

As he walked out of the classroom, he paused in the hallway. He looked down at the floor and quietly said, "This is the strangest start of summer break that I can ever remember."

2

As the rooster crowed, dawn was slowly approaching. Luke was already up, sitting on the front porch, drinking his morning cup of hot tea. It was his daily ritual. Not that he wasn't old enough to drink coffee, there just wasn't anything that tasted as good as hot tea with cream and sugar to get the day started. Besides, coffee left a bad taste in his mouth that he could hardly get rid of.

Before the sun had shone its full face, Luke had already eaten breakfast, fed the animals, and was on his way to rouse Josh to join him on an early morning trip to their favorite fishing spot. As he walked along the fence at Josh's, he looked for any signs of life stirring at the Johnson's house. Josh wasn't an early riser like himself. Heck, Josh could sleep all day if he could find an excuse for not having to crawl out of bed.

Luke heard a screen door slam. He walked around the side of the house in time to see Mr. Johnson carrying a bucket of water toward the barn.

"Hey, Mr. Johnson!" Luke called.

Not expecting to encounter anyone so early in the morning, Luke startled him. He swung around quickly, causing half of the water in the bucket to slosh out.

"L-Luke, I wasn't expecting, uh, what are you doing here this early?"

"Sorry, Mr. Johnson. Didn't mean to scare you like that. Just came to see if Josh wanted to go fishing."

"That's okay, Luke. Kind of made my heart jump into second gear. Guess I shouldn't be so jumpy. I doubt very seriously if Josh is awake. It would take an army to get him out of bed this early, but go on in and try if you want to."

"Thanks, Mr. Johnson."

Luke sat his fishing pole by the side door and walked into the kitchen. Mrs. Johnson was fixing breakfast and paid no attention to him.

"Hello, Mrs. Johnson," said Luke.

She looked up over the top of her glasses and smiled quizzically.

"Morning, Lucas. You come to get Josh or just to get a free breakfast?" she said, grinning out of one side of her mouth.

"No, ma'am. I mean, yes, ma'am. I mean, no, ma'am, I already ate, but yes, ma'am, I came to see if Josh wanted to go fishing."

"Sure, go ahead and wake him. I'm sure he'd like to go if you can get him up."

Luke opened the door to Josh's room. He called his name, but there was no response. He started to walk into the room and kicked something lying on the floor. With a loud thud, a baseball bounced off the wall and rolled over to the bed.

"Hmmm," Josh groaned.

"Josh, it's me, Luke. Want to go fishing?"

There was no answer. Apparently, it wasn't enough to awaken him. Just enough to interrupt his deep slumber and long enough for him to turn over and drift back asleep. Luke knew this was going to be no easy task. He shook Josh hard enough to register on the Richter scale. Josh's eyes opened, and he laid there for a few seconds staring at Luke. He rubbed his eyes, yawned, scratched his head, and smiled.

"Hey, Luke, what's up?"

"Just came by to see if you wanted to go fishing?"

"Sure, but all you had to do was holler, and I'd have gotten right up."

Luke looked at him, smiled, and rolled his eyes.

"Let's go, Josh. It's getting late."

"Okay, be ready in a minute."

Luke walked out of the room and back into the kitchen where Mrs. Johnson was almost finished making breakfast. The smell of fresh baked biscuits was almost too impossible to pass up. Luke knew that Josh would want to eat before heading out, so he kind of lolled around the breakfast table waiting for him. Anyway, Luke knew Mrs. Johnson would reaffirm her offer for him to have a bite to eat. And who could turn down fresh, hot biscuits? Besides, Mrs. Johnson's biscuits were known throughout the county as those tear-apart, aroma-filled, melt-in-your-mouth cakes of joy. It was too late now. There was no turning back. If she offered again, he would definitely indulge in this stomach-satisfying, palate-pleasing cuisine placed before him.

"Luke, LUCAS!"

"Y-yes, ma'am."

"Are you okay? You had your nose stuck way up in the air. Thought maybe you had a nosebleed, son."

"No, ma'am. I'm okay."

He liked when she called him son. She was like a second mother to him. Not that anyone could ever replace his own mother (she was the best there was), but if he did have another, he wished it would be Mrs. Johnson.

Luke didn't realize Josh was already sitting at the table staring at him with a puzzled look. He already had one biscuit buttered and was starting on the second.

"You sure you're okay, Luke?" said Josh.

"Sure, I was just thinking about something."

Mrs. Johnson smiled and said, "Luke, why don't you sit down and help Josh finish off those biscuits?"

Luke thought she would never ask. By the time the boys finished, eight biscuits had disappeared, along with a quart of milk. They were fuller than two pigs running loose in a slop house.

"We better get going, Josh. Once the sun gets too high, the fish won't be biting."

They headed out the door, along a dusty road, and onto a path that cut through the woods. This was their shortcut to their fishing spot on the lake. The brush was so thick that no one ever took the time to see where the path led (except of course Luke and Josh).

"Whew, these weeds have really grown a lot since last year," said Luke.

By the time the boys made it to their fishing spot, the sun was high, and they were tired and sweating. As they approached the lake, they noticed some of the weeds had been trampled and uprooted. Some of the trees had gashes, and there were numerous animal tracks.

"Hogs, Josh."

"Huh," said Josh.

"Hogs. They're rutting. Those are boar marks on those trees. They're marking their territory."

The boys stood there staring at the badly scarred trees, then at each other and around to see if there was any company close by.

"Josh, we need to keep our eyes open. If a momma sow comes around and she has little ones, she's not gonna be very happy to see us. And God forbid we cross paths with an old male boar. They're meaner than a rabid dog," said Luke. Not that he had ever seen a rabid dog, but from what he had heard, nothing could be as mean as a male boar. Funny thing was you didn't have to do anything to make them mad. They were just like that.

Josh's eyes opened twice their size. "What do you want to do, Luke?"

"Well, we came this far. Might as well get some fishing done," said Luke.

They started unpacking their fishing gear when they heard a huffing sound behind them. They quickly turned, straightened up, and stared with their mouths gaped wide open at an enormous sow charging toward them. She wasn't there to greet them hello. Behind her were four piglets doing all they could to keep up with her. She was snorting and squealing and raising all kinds of dust. The boys knew they had to do something quick. But where would they go? There was only brush, thick with briars, mostly surrounding them. No trees close enough to climb. They looked at each other and realized there was only one thing to do. They took one look at the water and plunged off the bank into the lake. The sow stopped just short of the water, shaking her head and kicking her hind legs. She pranced and strutted around in a circle for a few minutes, stopped, looked at her quarry, and realized there was nothing else she could do. She trotted off into the bushes with her head held high, piglets all in a row right behind her.

"That was close," Josh said.

"Yeah, too close," said Luke.

They looked out across the lake.

"Well, I don't think we're going to catch anything now. We done scared everything away," said Luke.

"That's okay. I don't feel much like fishing anyway. How are we going to get home?" questioned Josh.

Luke stood there in the waist-high water as if he were hypnotized. He looked around the lake. It was too big for them to swim across. He thought about hollering but doubted anyone would hear them. This time of the day was too hot for anyone to be in a boat. He thought about their secret path, but it was so narrow that if they ran into the sow, there would be nowhere to turn. Then, while looking up at the tall trees in the distance, it dawned on him. They were enormous, old hardwood trees so thickly rooted and overlapping that there shouldn't be any trouble supporting their weight. All they had to do was scale an old oak tree a ways down the bank and cross from one tree to another. At least that way, they could get a good distance from the lake before getting down and making a run for it. The boys talked it over and decided it was pretty much their only option, unless they wanted to sit in the lake all day and wrinkle up like a couple of prunes.

After gathering up their fishing gear, they made a mad dash for an old oak tree near the bank, about thirty yards away. Luke climbed up onto a low-hanging limb. Josh handed Luke the fishing rods and tackle, then hurriedly jumped up onto the limb, cautiously looking back for any sign of Mrs. Piggy.

"Okay, Josh, let's get going," said Luke.

It was a slow process. Luke climbing and crawling from one tree to the next, retrieving the fishing gear from Josh, then moving out of the way while Josh made his way over. Then they would split up the gear and move toward the next tree. Over and over they went until their hands were sore and raw. Finally, they came to the last tree near the path. It wasn't as large as the other trees and was questionable whether the limbs were large enough to hold the both of them, but there was no other option. The limbs of the tree they were sitting on were too high off the ground for them to jump down.

"Looks like we're gonna have to go for it, Josh," said Luke. Once I cross over, I should be able to climb down low enough to get the weight off those limbs."

Once Luke secured himself in the tree, Josh was able to hand him the fishing rods. He wasn't able to get close enough to hand Luke the tackle box.

"Josh, you're going to have to throw it to me."

"I don't know if I can reach you," said Josh.

"Don't worry. If it falls, it can always be replaced. Just give it your best shot."

"Okay, on three," said Josh.

Josh heaved the tackle box toward Luke. It was a little out of his reach, but he was able to lean toward the tree just as the box crashed into the bark. He maintained his balance as he grabbed ahold of it. The crash caused a large crack in the side of the tackle box, but the clasp and hinges were intact.

Luke breathed a sigh of relief as he sat upright with the box securely in his arms.

"Okay, Josh, come on over."

"Be right there."

Once Josh made it to the tree where Luke was waiting, they rested for a few minutes. Luke held onto the tackle box and handed the fishing rods to Josh.

"We ought to be able to run for it after we get down from this tree," said Luke.

"You sure we're far enough?" asked Josh.

"Gonna have to be. Ain't no other trees close enough to the path unless you want to run through the bushes to get there."

"Yeah, I guess so," Josh said hesitantly.

Looking up the pathway, it was obvious that it was getting late. The shadows that were cast across the path brought a renewed sense of fear. Their eyes raced back and forth looking for any sign of movement from the dark silhouettes. They just knew the old sow was waiting in the shadows for her chance to finish them off. At least that's what their imaginations had dreamed up.

Mrs. Meyers was getting concerned about the boys. It wasn't like Luke to be gone fishing all day long. He was usually home by early afternoon to eat lunch. Her mind began to wander. Luke and Josh were probably playing some kind of game and didn't realize the time. Yeah, that was probably it. She waited a little while longer and decided to call the Johnsons' to see if the boys were there, but talking to Mrs. Johnson offered no relief. She hadn't seen the boys since early that morning at the breakfast table. Now Mrs. Johnson was starting to worry too. Sarah hung up the phone and looked out the window.

Darn that boy, she thought.

"Henry, HENRY!"

"You think we ought to go look for the boys?"

"Nah, they'll be along soon. Heck, a boy with a fishing pole is like a woman with a new baby. Neither one wants to put it down. Just relax."

"You don't suppose anything—Oh, you don't worry about anything, do you, Henry?"

Henry knew the more she fretted, the faster her imagination would run. He realized it was time to go look for the boys. By the tone of her voice, it was obvious she was worried and just needed the reassurance that her son was alright. Besides, he knew dinner would be delayed with Sarah looking out the window every five seconds. And he was hungry!

"Okay, when I get out of the tree, you throw the rods and tackle box down. If I drop the box or it spills, it doesn't matter. It ain't that important. We just need to hurry," said Luke.

"I'm ready," said Josh.

"Me too, let's go."

As soon as Luke was on the ground, Josh tossed the supplies right on top of him. He quickly picked up everything that was in arm's reach. Josh slid down the tree like a fireman on a firepole. They grabbed everything they could and ran as if that old sow was right behind them. Needless to say, she wasn't, but they weren't about to look back to see. By the time they reached the main road, they were panting and wheezing so hard they could hardly speak. They stopped, caught their breath, looked at each other, laughed, and headed home.

Henry put his shoes on, grabbed his hat, and fumbled through his pockets for the car keys. With his limited sight, he didn't drive much, especially when it was getting late. But because of the circumstances, he knew he had to do something.

Hmm, I know I had them last night, he thought to himself.

"Honey, have you seen the car keys? I can't seem to find them."

"They're right on the end table by the newspaper, where you always leave them."

Sure enough, that's exactly where they were.

"What would I do without you to always help me find the car keys?"

"You'd be doing a lot of walking instead of driving," said Sarah.

"I guess you're right," he chuckled.

Henry was on his way out the back door when he spotted Luke walking up the road, head down with his fishing rod on his right shoulder.

"Well, here's your little outdoorsman now," he said to Sarah as he headed back inside to the living room and his favorite chair.

She smiled and breathed a deep sigh. She tried not to sound overanxious, as if she wasn't worried at all.

"So it is" was all she said as she went back to cooking.

Luke sat his fishing rod and tackle box on the back porch and walked through the kitchen toward his room without saying a word. Mrs. Meyers was at the stove. She turned, looked at him, then went back to stirring the food in the pot. She did a quick double take and took a deep breath.

"Lucas, what on earth happened to you? You look like you've been dragged through a cow pasture. Did you catch any fish?"

"No, ma'am, they weren't biting."

"Well, you better get cleaned up. Supper's almost ready."

"Mom, is it alright if I skip dinner tonight?"

"I can't recall you ever missing supper, son. Are you sure you're okay?"

"Yes, ma'am. I'm just kind of tired. It's been a really long day."

Luke walked into his bedroom, took his shoes and clothes off, and crawled into bed. He didn't even take time to get cleaned up. Apparently, he felt that floating in the lake as long as he did was close enough to a bath for one day. After a few seconds, he was sound asleep, and he didn't wake up until the next morning when the sun was coming through the shades of his windows.

3

Summer was easing by, and the Meyers were getting ready to harvest their crops. Nothing automatic, no fancy machinery, just old-fashioned labor. Besides, with the three of them working morning and evening, they could finish in about a week. It had been a dry spring, and summer wasn't promising to be any better. The crops were beginning to parch, showing signs of stress. If they weren't picked soon, there would be little to salvage. It was hard enough keeping the crows from getting their fill. "Patches" (Luke was proud of the name he had picked out), the old scarecrow Henry had erected to scare the birds away, had slowly deteriorated through the years. The birds didn't even feel threatened anymore. They sat on his outstretched arms and cackled in unison as if making fun of what once was but is no more.

As the sun set and night descended on their small farm, the Meyers were preparing for their harvest.

"Luke, we're going to start picking in the morning, son," said Mr. Meyers. "We need to get to bed early so we can get started before sunrise. I'm not as young as I used to be. That heat is almost too much for me after ten in the morning. We'll take a rest until it cools off. Probably around five. Is that okay with you, son?"

"Sure, Dad. Whatever you think."

Luke liked that his dad asked for his opinion. It made him feel important to be included in the decision-making.

"See you in the morning, son."

"Night, Luke," said his mom.

"Night, Mom, Dad."

Luke lay in bed listening to the sounds of the night. As usual, for a boy his age, his mind was full of adventures and questions. He wondered about Mrs. Cargood's boy. Until his dad mentioned it, nobody had ever said a word about her losing a son. But then everyone was too scared to even talk to her. *I guess they just didn't understand her*, he thought. Soon he was off to sleep. When he opened his eyes, he could smell the aroma of bacon. He turned on his side, sniffed, rubbed his nose, threw the covers back, and rolled out of bed. He staggered into the kitchen, hands shielding his eyes, trying to let them focus in the light.

"Morning, Luke," his mom said. "Your plate's on the table."

Mr. Meyers was already in the barn preparing their makeshift harvesting buckets. Actually, they were gunnysacks with a rope attached to each side of the open end. The rope was to fit over the head and rest on one shoulder while the sack was saddled across the hip. This left the arms free to pick and fill the sack with a constant rhythm.

After breakfast, they donned their harvesting clothes and started the tedious task. They worked side by side, hardly taking a break until the sun made it too hot to go on. Henry reached for one more corn shuck before starting toward the house. As he bent down, Luke let out a scream that would curl your hair.

"Dad, look out!"

"Wh-what the—?"

Luke's foot slammed down hard on the ground, barely missing his dad's fingers. Henry looked on in bewilderment as the dark body of a snake writhed under the pressure of Luke's boot. This time of the year, gardens were a prime area for snakes. The crops helped shade them from the sun. This particular one was a copperhead. One bite surely meant a trip to the hospital.

"That was close, son. I didn't even see it. I sure am glad you were here. Let's get rid of it and go take a break."

Henry's heart was still racing as he and Luke walked back toward the house. As he wiped his forehead with a rag, he noticed dark clouds gathering to the west.

"Well, I'll be. Looks like we may finally get some relief from this heat," he said to himself.

When Henry walked into the kitchen, Sarah was busy fixing some sandwiches. The radio was playing in the background. Without looking up or pausing from her task, she calmly and without emotion said, "Storm's a-coming."

"Huh? What's that?" said Henry.

"That's what the weatherman said. Storm's a-coming. Said it's a big one. Flooding up the country a ways."

Henry looked out the window and could see the clouds were getting closer. He hollered at Luke to make sure the horse and cows were tied up in the barn and the pens secured. If a storm was coming, the last thing he needed was to be out in it chasing down animals. Besides, storms could get pretty rough in this part of the country. They lived on the edge of what is considered "Tornado Alley." Over the years, they had seen firsthand the wrath of Mother Nature. Too much rain or wind could be just as devastating on the crops as no rain at all.

Henry trudged back out to the garden to work a little more before the rains came. Soon, Luke joined him, and together they worked like a finely tuned machine. They were tired, but there was no stopping. Once the rain set in, it could be a day or two before they would be able to pick again.

Henry raised his head and took a deep breath. The smell of rain was unmistakable. It was getting closer. The winds were starting to pick up. It was time to stop, get the family together, and head for the cellar. Sarah was finishing up in the kitchen. She gathered enough food and drink to get them through the evening (even if it meant spending the night in the cellar, which had been done many times). They headed for the safety vault.

The winds were really blowing hard now. The tall loblolly pines were bending so far it seemed they could snap at any second. Henry opened the cellar door and waited for Luke and Sarah to get in. As he was pulling the door shut, he could hear it—that eerie, distinct sound of a freight train. But a train it wasn't. There was no mistaking it. A tornado! He paused to look up at the sky. At that split second, a huge gust yanked the door from his hand and almost off the hinges. He tried to reach for it, but the wind was too strong. He was being pelted by debris. The force was too powerful, and he wasn't about to waste time fighting back. A rope attached to the door handle was whipping about madly. Henry made one last effort and grabbed the rope. His foot slipped, and he fell forward into the opening onto the stairs. Still clutching the rope, he pulled with all his strength until the door slammed shut. In one motion, he pulled himself up and wrapped the rope around a nail on the jamb and secured the latch.

Henry hurried down the stairs to the far corner where his family crouched. They knew the drill. Through the years, it had been put to the test time and time again. The blowing wind and steady rain eventually put Luke to sleep in the warm comfort of his mother's arms. When he woke, it was dark. The air was quiet except for an occasional clap of thunder in the distance. They had weathered another storm.

After daybreak, they would survey the damage and start the tedious task of repair or replace.

At the first sign of dawn, Henry opened the cellar door and stepped out onto the rain-soaked ground. He did a complete three-sixty, pausing at certain intervals with a mesmerizing stare. Miraculously enough, everything seemed to be intact except for the tops of some of the pine trees. They looked as if something had twisted them and chewed the bark off. He knew what that "something" was. The garden had survived, except now most of the vegetables were on the ground instead of on the plants. This meant they would have to get busy picking up their bounty. Once the vegetables were on the ground, they would not survive long being submerged in the water and mud. This would make it harder on their backs to continuously stay bent over. Nevertheless, it wasn't going to get done by standing there and looking. They quickly got started, and in no time their bags were full. It was midmorning, and already, the stooping was taking its toll.

"I think this would be a good time to take a break," said Henry.

"Sounds good to me," said Sarah.

Luke didn't say anything. He plodded silently back toward the house. The lack of sleep the night before and the laborious work was taking its toll on him. Luke heard someone holler his name. He turned, looked down the road a distance, and saw Josh coming his way on his bike at full speed. When Josh neared, he put on the brakes hard enough to make the bike slide sideways on the muddy ground. The bike stopped just short of running into Luke.

"What's the matter, Josh?"

"Nothing. Just wanted to see if you wanted to take a ride down the road. A big ole oak tree fell across a car last night during the storm. They may need some help moving it. Wanna go?"

Luke took a deep breath. "Well, I'd like to, but we're picking the garden right now."

"Can't you take a break?"

Luke scratched his head. He was tired, but a bike ride would be a welcome change.

"Well, let me ask my dad."

Luke hollered out, "Hey, Dad, can I go with Josh to see a tree that fell across a car last night?"

"Sure, go ahead, son. You've earned it. Be careful, and don't be too late. We need to get some more work done this evening."

"Okay, I won't be long."

As the boys pedaled down the road, they passed an old sign nailed to a pine tree. It read County Cemetery. Luke thought about the story his dad had told him about Mrs. Cargood's son. He wondered if that's where he was buried. Maybe sometimes he would go see for himself. While he daydreamed, he slowly fell farther behind Josh.

"Hey, Luke, what's the matter? Something wrong with your bike?"

"Huh, oh, no, it's okay. Just thinking about something."

"Well, come on. We're almost there."

As the boys approached the fallen tree, the car was hardly visible. The old oak was so large it almost completely covered the vehicle.

"Wow," said Josh.

Luke looked on in amazement. "It's a good thing nobody was in it. They'd be flat as a pancake."

The boys stood there and watched as people were already cutting limbs and using chain saws to dissect sections of the tree. After being uprooted in the storm, the demise of the old Goliath was imminent. It was almost sad to see, but by cutting it up, it ensured a quick death—no lingering, no decay. It would be used for firewood in the wintertime. All that would be left of the old tree would be memories of where it stood and of course a hole in the ground where the roots had called home for many, many years. As the scavengers (or so it seemed that way to Luke) were busy salvaging parts of the tree (like vultures feasting on a newly discovered meal), the excitement quickly wore off. Luke and Josh headed home. Josh turned off at his house. They exchanged waves, leaving Luke to ride home the rest of the way by himself. Once again, Luke started daydreaming about the cemetery sign. Before he knew it, he was sitting on his bike in front of his house. When he snapped out of it, he looked back at the road in disbelief. He didn't remember his trip home after waving goodbye to Josh. Once again, his daydreaming had engulfed him to the point that he was not aware of his surroundings. A kind of eerie feeling came upon him. "What if I would have been in the path of an oncoming car while I was in the middle of the road? I wouldn't have even seen it." He felt kind of sick and realized he had better start paying attention to what he was doing.

When Luke walked into the house, his dad questioned him about the old tree that had fallen. He didn't elaborate much on it and acted like it was no big deal. He asked his dad about the old cemetery sign he saw along the road. Hearing the word *cemetery*, his mom looked around from her sewing room and asked why he was interested in that. "Oh, nothing really. I was just wondering if that's where Mrs. Cargood's son was buried?"

"Well, a cemetery is no place for a boy your age to go snooping around. You stay away from there, you hear?" his mother said sternly.

"Yes, ma'am, I will."

Luke walked away, still not satisfied. *There has to be a way to find out*, Luke thought. He knew not to go there, though, especially after his mom said not to. He didn't want to think about what would happen if he disobeyed her. It wouldn't be pleasant. He dropped it at that. At least for the time being.

After a long day working in the garden and riding his bike, Luke had no problem falling asleep that night.

4

The harvesting had finally come to an end. After a week of picking vegetables (from the plants and off the ground) morning and evening, Luke didn't care if he saw any corn, tomatoes, squash, or cucumbers ever again. At least not until he was hungry. He walked outside to the barn to feed the animals and saw his dad separating the vegetables into separate piles.

"Hey, Dad, need a hand?"

"No, I'm okay. It doesn't look like there's going to be a whole lot here to keep."

"What do you mean?"

"Well, son, it looks as if the heat and lack of rain took its toll on the crops. The corn and tomatoes didn't fully develop, and a lot of the squash is starting to rot. All that work and not much to show for it." Henry shook his head.

"It's going to be okay, Dad."

"I'm sure it will be, son. Oh well, no use crying over spoiled vegetables." Henry grinned. "Now that we're finished, why don't you start enjoying the rest of your summer."

"Thanks, Dad. I'm going to finish feeding the animals, then I'm going to see what Josh is doing."

Josh had been stopping by each day wanting Luke to play ball, ride bikes, or maybe camp out, but each time, Luke had declined; not that he didn't want to, but he knew his parents were depending on him to help. It was a full-time job that required "early to bed and early to rise." But now, all that had changed. Luke was ready to have some fun. He called Josh to see if he was ready for a camp over.

"Are you kidding? I'm so bored. I'll be there in a few minutes."

"Okay, but don't forget to bring your glove."

Luke was getting some of his things together when Josh walked into his room.

"Hey, Luke."

"Wow, that was quick. Help me find my flash-light, and I think that'll be it."

As the boys walked through the living room, Mr. Meyers looked up from his newspaper, gave a polite smile, and went back to reading. They walked into the kitchen and loaded up some goodies. They were almost out the door when Mrs. Meyers called to them. "What are you boys plans for the evening?"

"Mmm, going outside to set up a tent and camp out. We're going to hang out and tell stories. You know, guy things."

"Hmm. Okay, well you *guys* don't go getting into any trouble."

"We won't. See you in the morning."

The boys didn't waste any time setting up their makeshift tent. A rope tied between two trees with an old blanket thrown over the rope, stretched out into an upside-down V, and secured to the ground at each corner. They threw their things on the ground inside the tent.

"Want to throw the baseball, Josh?"

"Sure."

As they tired of throwing the ball, they decided to get into the tent and tell stories. Like most boys their age, the stories were made up on the spot. Nothing true. Designed to make you wonder when it's dark and you hear a noise outside the tent. Do you go look or just pull the covers over your head and go to sleep? Then Luke thought about the cemetery.

"Hey, Josh, you ever hear that Mrs. Cargood had a son that died?"

Josh had a puzzled look on his face. "A son? A son that died?"

Luke rolled his eyes. "Yeah, that's what I said."

"Heck, I didn't know she was married."

"Well, she ain't no more. But that's a long story. Anyway, I heard about it and was wondering if anyone else knew about it."

"No, I never heard that."

Luke knew it was true. If his dad told him something, there was no second-guessing. His curiosity to see for himself was starting to get the best of him.

"You ever been over to the County Cemetery, Josh?"

"No, I can't say that I have. I've passed by it plenty of times, but never had no urge to go there. Why, what are you getting at?" he hesitantly asked.

"Well, I was just thinking. My mom doesn't want me hanging out around there. But if we just went and came right back, that would be different."

"I don't know, Luke. I don't really see the difference. I don't think we ought to be going there. Especially at night."

"It won't take long. It's just up the road a bit. I just gotta see for myself if he's there."

Josh scratched his head and looked at Luke with an expression of uneasiness. "I guess, but let's hurry. I don't want to hang around there too long."

Luke knew Josh wasn't thrilled with the idea, and he hated doing something his mom had told him not to do, but something just kept telling him he needed to go see for himself. Besides, what could it really hurt? They grabbed their flashlights, hopped on their bikes and were at the entrance road to the cemetery in no time. They stopped and looked at the old County Cemetery sign. If the dilapidated old sign was any indication of how the cemetery was maintained, they had their work cut out for them. The weeds had probably overgrown the deteriorated old headstones. They waited for a few seconds, listening for any sign of company. Other than a symphony of crickets and an occasional frog warming his vocal cords, it was pretty safe to say they were alone.

"Okay, Josh, let's go see what we can find."

"Sure, but let's hurry. I don't think my mom would be too happy either if she knew where I was."

They pedaled down the dark winding road about a quarter of a mile until they came to an opening. The half-moon illuminated the cemetery just enough for them to see the entrance gate.

From what they could see, the cemetery was actually in better shape than they had envisioned.

"Got your flashlight, Josh? Let's get started."

5

Mrs. Meyers decided to fix the boys some hot chocolate. She knew they would be up late talking about Lord knows what, and a good warm cup of cocoa would be the perfect nightcap. She called out the back door for the boys but got no response. *Hmm. Maybe they slipped by me. They could be in Luke's room*, she thought. Walking back through the kitchen, she looked around the corner down the hall at Luke's room. The light was off, and the door was open. Still nothing to worry about. With a barn, storage building, and fifteen acres of land, those two could be just about anywhere. She called out the back door again for the boys.

"Luke, Josh. Got some hot cocoa for you. It's getting cold."

Still no response. She stood in the doorway, her eyes fixated on the tree line toward the back of the property. If they were out there, they for sure would have flashlights. Scanning for anything, she saw no movement or lights. Nothing. Now maybe there was reason for concern.

The boys no sooner got started when in the distance, they could hear the sound of a vehicle. They froze in their tracks, looking at each other.

"Could be a car passing on the highway," said Josh.

They listened for a few more seconds. No, the sound was getting louder. Someone was coming! The boys knew they had better find a place to hide quick. Running toward the back corner of the cemetery, Luke remembered the bikes.

"Geez, Josh, the bikes. If they see 'em, they'll know someone's here."

Both boys were starting to sweat now. Beads of perspiration rolling down their foreheads. There wasn't time to maneuver the bikes through all the headstones, so they decided to lay them down behind a large crypt. At least their bikes would be out of direct sight. They made it to the back corner and ducked behind an large old obelisk headstone just as the car pulled up, its lights casting shadows of the grave markers. The lights stayed on for what seemed an eternity. Then the car started backing up. The lights went off, but they could still hear the engine. The car stopped at the back of the cemetery, about thirty feet from where they were hiding. They looked at each other with gaping mouths, knowing at any second, they would be spotted.

Then the engine shut off. There was an eerie silence. The boys lay there, still as statues, barely hearing themselves breathe. The car just sat there. No sound of a door opening. Whoever it was, was just sitting there, waiting. Luke leaned over to Josh and whispered in his ear.

"I wonder why someone would be out here this late at night?"

Josh cocked his head sideways and whispered back to Luke, "Duh, I'm sure if they see us, they'll be thinking the same thing."

Luke rolled over and looked around the corner of the headstone. To his amazement, it was a police car. It was parked at an angle not facing them. He could barely make out the silhouette of the officer sitting in the car, a cup and a bag on the dashboard.

The policeman slumped down in his seat, picked up the cup, and started sipping on its contents. Apparently, he planned to be there awhile.

Luke pushed himself back behind the grave.

"What'd you see?" whispered Josh.

"It's a policeman, and he looks like he's waiting for someone."

"Who'd he be waiting for way out here?"

"I don't know, but it looks like he's not going anywhere for a while."

"What are we going to do, Luke?"

"Heck, I dunno. Maybe he'll leave soon. Let's wait 'n' see."

The boys lay back on the ground, staring at the stars in the sky. Not the most comforting place to marvel at Mother Nature, but they weren't going anywhere anytime soon.

Mrs. Meyers was now to the point of worrying. It was nearing midnight, and still no sign of Luke and Josh. The hot had gone out of the cocoa hours ago. Knowing boys their age liked to explore, she wanted to give them the benefit of the doubt, but her patience was about stretched to the limit. Calling Josh's parents and waking them at this hour was a last resort, but the thought of something happening to the boys was overwhelming.

Luke rolled over again and peeked around the corner at the police car. When his eyes focused, he could see the officer was slumped forward. His hat was pulled down over his eyes. He was heaving up and down with every breath. Sound asleep! Luke breathed a sigh of relief.

"This is it, Josh. He's asleep. Let's get outa here!"

They stood up in a crouched position, and started easing their way toward their bikes.

"Wh-what the?" Luke quietly said.

They froze. Noticing two figures coming through the cemetery entrance, they squatted down where they were standing, out in the open but stiff as boards. The two figures veered toward the right. Luke could barely make them out but could tell they were men and carrying something. They stopped near the back, on the opposite side of the cemetery, and knelt down. After a few seconds, their arms began to move back and forth. Luke and Josh weren't sure what was going on. All of a sudden, they realized what it was. They looked at each other, and without saying a word, their eyes said it all. "Looters! Grave robbers!" Now they began to panic. They knew this was no place to be, especially in the middle of the night.

"Think! Think! What are we going to do?" Luke pondered.

About that time, a deep voice in a low whisper said, "What on earth are you two boys doing here?" They turned white and nearly passed out but turned and saw Chief Ramsey crouched behind them. Apparently, they were so busy keeping an eye on the thieves, they didn't even hear the chief get out of his car. But he saw them!

"I want you boys to stay right here. Don't move. I've been looking for these two for a couple of months."

Chief Ramsey crawled on his hands and knees until he was fairly close to the grave robbers. They were busy digging and were unaware that anyone was nearby. The chief drew his gun, turned on his flashlight, and caught them red-handed. One of them appeared to reach for something, but relaxed his hand after Chief Ramsey, with his bass voice said, "I don't think you want to do that." He told them to sit up on their knees. He threw a pair of handcuffs on the ground between them and had one of them handcuff the other. Then he restrained the other one. He frisked each one and found a small-caliber handgun under the shirt of one of them. As he escorted them back to his patrol car, they passed within a few feet of Luke and Josh who were still motionless, just as the chief had instructed.

As they passed by, Luke's eyes got as big as saucers. *It's them! The two men from Henley's store. So that's why they were getting shovels in the store.*

49

His heart was beating hard. He wanted to tell Josh about them, but he kept quiet. Just then, one of the looters turned his head and spit in the direction of Luke. He looked up. His walk slowed. His neck jutted out to get a better look at who was standing there. His eyes narrowed then opened wide. "You! What are you—?"

The chief cut him off, "Keep quiet, and keep moving."

After Chief Ramsey had the two men securely in the car, he returned to talk to Luke and Josh. Luke knew this wasn't going to be good.

"What was that all about?" the chief asked.

"I-I don't know," said Luke. I may have seen them before. Luke knew. He was just too scared and didn't want to get involved. Little did he know that he and Josh were already involved.

Chief Ramsey was a huge man, about six feet, three inches. You could not mistake his voice. It was not overly loud, but very deep and smooth. When he talked, people knew to listen. He had been the police chief for as long as Luke could remember.

"I don't know what possessed you boys to be out here in the cemetery at this time of the night, but… I've been trying to catch these thieves for a long time. You could have botched this up for me, or worse, you could have gotten yourselves hurt. Either of you want to explain?"

Luke hesitantly spoke up. "This is all my fault, sir." Luke told him about the campout and about Mrs. Cargood's son and how he just wanted to see for himself if he was buried there. When he finished, there was a long silence. Then Chief Ramsey took a deep breath and exhaled. He rubbed his forehead and said, "This is probably a silly question, but do your parents know where you are?"

"No, sir. In fact, my mother told me before to stay away from here."

"That's what I thought. I'm sure they're worried sick about you boys. How did you get out here?"

"We rode our bikes. We hid them when we heard someone coming," said Josh.

"I see. Follow me."

I knew it, thought Luke. *This is when it's going to get bad.*

Luke and Josh followed behind the chief with their heads down, not knowing what was coming next. Chief Ramsey stopped in the middle of the cemetery, didn't say a word, just pointed to a headstone. The boys bent down and tried to make out the name inscribed on the headstone. The chief turned on his flashlight and illuminated the inscription. It read, "Kyle Cargood—Our Little Angel." They stared at it for a few seconds, then Luke started getting this strange feeling. *What's wrong with me?* he thought. It felt like there was a baseball lodged in his throat.

"Luke! Lucas!" the chief called.

"Huh, what?"

"Are you okay, son?"

"Yes, sir. I'm fine." Luke's eyes were full of tears (like a dam ready to release water). He turned away and wiped his eyes on his shirt.

"Must have gotten something in my eye. It's okay now."

"Okay, let's go," said the chief.

Luke and Josh hesitated and looked at each other. Apparently, Chief Ramsey picked up on what they were thinking. "Don't worry, boys, I'm not putting you in the car with those two. Technically you haven't done anything wrong."

Boy that was a relief, the boys thought.

"But I want you to get on your bikes and get straight home! No more of these nighttime shenanigans. You boys understand?"

"Yes, sir," they both said.

"Good! I trust both of you at your word."

"Thanks, Chief Ramsey," Luke said, feeling a little ashamed and embarrassed.

The chief got in and started the squad car. He waited and made sure the boys were on their bikes and heading home, then sped off. He radioed the station and notified the on-duty dispatcher, Wanda Brown, that he had two 10-15's (suspects in custody), and he would require a 10-34 (assistance) when he arrived. She asked for his 10-20 (location), and he responded that he was on Gizzler Road about ten to twelve minutes out. The dispatcher acknowledged 10-4 (okay), then the radio went silent.

Luke and Josh looked at each other with relief, knowing things could have been a lot worse. *What if Chief Ramsey had not been there and the robbers had spotted them*, each thought. They tried not to think about it, but it kept coming back to them. They pedaled as hard and fast as they could. It only took about ten minutes to get home.

The chief pulled up to the back of the police station and radioed a request for a 10-99 (open police overhead garage door). This is where most prisoners were brought in to be processed and booked. Not that there were many criminals in this sleepy little town, but instead of parading them through the front door, it helped keep a sense of comfort in the community. It's like the old cliché "out of sight, out of mind." He eased the car inside, and the overhead door closed. He was met there by Officer Emmett Kirk. The chief told Officer Kirk the prisoners had been read their rights, so take them downstairs and lock them up. He would have to deal with them in the morning. It was already one in the morning, and the judge would not be available for arraignment until nine in the morning.

As he walked past dispatch, he stopped and asked Wanda if everything else was going okay tonight. She looked up from her magazine and assured him "all was quiet."

"Good, I'll be back in the morning. Have a good night."

"You too, hon," she said.

As he turned to leave, she said, "Oh, Jack, I almost forgot, Sarah Meyers called about a half hour ago. She said her son Luke and his friend Josh were camping out in their yard and she went to check on them and they were gone. She was wondering if you may have spotted them while on patrol. She sounded very upset."

He looked at his watch and noted that it was about a half hour ago when they were leaving the cemetery. He looked at Wanda and said, "I have a hunch she's already found them. But you may want to call her and confirm." Wanda grinned and said, "10-4 that." Chief Ramsey walked out the door and headed home.

When Luke and Josh pedaled their bikes into the yard, they noticed all the lights were on inside and outside the house.

Luke quietly said, "This isn't good. This time of the night, it should be pitch-black out here."

They stood there and noticed movement in the house. Mrs. Meyers walked past the kitchen window, and as if on cue, Mr. Meyers walked out of the barn, right up behind them.

"Where on earth have you two been?"

The boys froze, not knowing which one was going to answer, or if they even could.

"Luke, your mother is almost in tears. She's already called the police."

Luke was barely able to speak. "The police?"

Josh chimed in. "We were just out exploring. Riding up and down some of the old county roads."

"So, you say," Mr. Meyers said. "I'm not sure how much I'll be able to help you out of this one, boys."

Luke looked back toward the house just in time to see his mother standing in the doorway. She pushed the screen door open and started walking toward them. "Lucas Meyers!" she said. "Do you realize—" The phone rang. She paused midsentence, turned, and went to answer the phone. The phone was located by the kitchen door, and the boys were close enough to hear the conversation.

"Yes, this is Sarah. Hi, Wanda. Yes, the boys just showed up. Thank you for calling." She hung the phone up.

Mrs. Meyers did not come back outside. She walked to her bedroom.

"Hmm. Let me go talk to her, Luke," said his dad. "Why don't you boys turn in for the night, but this time stay in the tent, okay?"

"Yes, sir, we will," they both said.

They crawled into the tent, got into their sleeping bags, and didn't say anything for a few minutes. Finally, Luke said, "Did you hear my mom on the phone?"

"Yeah, I think so."

"It didn't sound like she was talking to the sheriff," said Luke.

"So."

"That means she doesn't know where we really were," said Luke.

Henry walked through the house looking for Sarah. He found her sitting in the bedroom on the side of the bed, staring at the floor.

"You okay, darling?"

Sarah nodded.

After a short silence, Sarah said, "I know I worry a lot, but he's still a boy, and he's all we have. If anything would ever happen to him—"

Henry interrupted her. "I know, Sarah, and I agree with you. He is a good boy."

This seemed to comfort her. She looked up at Henry and managed to give him a slight smile. Henry sat down beside her, put his arms around her, and gave her a tight hug.

"Thank you, Henry. You always know what I need."

"Let's get some sleep," said Henry. "The boys promised to stay in the tent the rest of the night. I'll talk to Luke in the morning.

6

The next morning, Chief Ramsey walked into the police station at 8:00 a.m. He was very punctual. Everything appeared to be business as usual. The smell of coffee was in the air, and he felt like he could drink an entire pot after the short night he had. He walked into his office to get his personal cup, one that he was proud of. It had been given to him years ago by the mayor, to honor him for all the years of dedicated service. He was highly appreciated by all his coworkers, and he felt the same about each one of them. He picked up his cup and noticed a folder laying on his desk. He opened it. Knowing what it contained, he gave it a quick once-over, closed it, and headed down the hall to fill his cup. The wheels were already in motion. He was already thinking about the names of the two men he arrested last night.

One of the officers on shift was standing at the coffee station. After exchanging greetings, the officer, Martin Gillman, offered to fill his cup.

"Thanks, Martin. Everything okay this morning?"

"Yes, sir."

"Prisoners behaving?"

"So far so good. One of them has asked about bail."

The chief grinned. "That doesn't surprise me. Thieves don't like being locked up. It keeps them from doing what they do best."

Officer Martin laughed. "Yeah that's true."

"Let me know if you need anything, Martin. I'll be in my office going over their paperwork." Chief Ramsey walked back to his office, sat down at his desk, and opened the folder. He stared at the names listed on the forms and took a big gulp of coffee. It burned going down, but he was used to it. One of the names rang a bell, but he couldn't put his finger on it. He picked up the phone and called the dispatch supervisor, Helen Parker.

"Morning, Helen."

"Morning, Jack."

"Helen, can you do me a favor?"

"Sure, Jack. What can I help you with?"

"Can you run a background check on the two prisoners I brought in last night?" He read her the names and birthdates of the two men. "Also, run it through the state database, and let me know what information you get."

"Consider it done. But it will probably take about an hour."

"That's fine. They aren't going anywhere."

7

Luke stared at the top of the tent. The sun was rising, and he had hardly slept a wink. He knew he had to tell his parents the truth. He'd never lied to them before, and he knew that if they found out from someone else, not only would he lose their trust, but probably his freedom for the rest of summer break, and there wasn't much of that left before school started.

Luke turned his head and looked over at Josh. Josh was staring straight at him.

"I don't think you've blinked in five minutes," said Josh.

"I'm going to tell them what happened last night," Luke said.

"Who?"

"My parents."

"When?" quizzed Josh.

"At breakfast."

Josh sat up. "Aw, can't it wait? I'm starving. I don't want to hear no yelling while I'm trying to eat. And besides, if they send you to your room, I'll be sittin' there by myself. Lord knows what will happen. I don't want them startin' in on me!"

"No, I need to get it out of the way," said Luke.

Josh disappointedly said, "Well, I've got some chores to do today, so I'll just eat at home. Good luck."

Luke didn't acknowledge Josh. He was too busy in deep thoughts about what he was going to say to his parents. He crawled out of the tent and slowly walked into the house.

Mrs. Meyers was just taking some biscuits out of the oven. She glanced at Luke and set the biscuits on the stove. His dad was already sitting at the table.

"Where's Josh?" asked his mom.

"He had some chores to do."

After a long pause, Luke hesitantly said, "Mom, Dad, there's something I need to tell you."

*****

It was now midmorning. Helen walked into the chief's office.

"Sorry it took so long."

"No problem," said Jack.

"Boy, you've got a couple of humdingers there. Rap sheets a mile long," Helen said.

She laid the papers down on his desk and turned around to walk out.

"Let me know it you need anything else."

"Thanks, Helen, I will."

Chief Ramsey perused the information of the first prisoner, Ed Toomey. Nothing really stood out, mostly petty crimes. He finished reading the list, put it aside, and moved on. He leaned back, put his feet up, and started scanning the information of the second prisoner, Butch Freeman. Nearly finished, he paused, looked up into the air, and thought to himself, *bingo*!

Butch Freeman was no small-time crook. About five years earlier, he was tied to a double homicide in a town in the southern part of the state. The story made national headlines. His brother was arrested for burglary of a bank. Two witnesses that were set to testify against him at his trial mysteriously disappeared. Another witness told authorities that he saw a man that looked similar to Butch near one of the witness's homes before he was reported missing. Freeman was arrested and questioned. But due to lack of evidence and witnesses, he and his brother were released. No money was ever recovered, and Butch Freeman hadn't been heard from until now.

Chief Ramsey finished his paperwork and sent it over to the courthouse for the judge to set a hearing date. Later that day, he received word the judge had set the arraignment for the next day at 9:00 a.m. The chief called Officer Jones into his office.

"Hey, Emmitt, can you let Freeman and Toomey know their court date is set for tomorrow morning at 9:00 a.m.?"

"Sure thing," said Emmitt.

"I'm heading home. I need to get a good night's sleep. Tomorrow will probably be very interesting. Let me know if you need anything."

"Will do," Emmitt said.

Instead of going straight home, Chief Ramsey had one stop to make, Lucas Meyers's house. It wasn't to make sure that Luke had told his parents about the night in the cemetery. It was to give them a heads-up about the possibility that Butch Freeman and his accomplice would get out on bail. They probably had nothing to worry about, but given the background of those two, they all needed to be on guard.

The chief pulled up to the Meyers' house. Sarah heard the sound of a vehicle and pushed a curtain aside to see who it was.

"Henry, the police are here!

"Wh-what?" muttered Henry.

Henry jumped to his feet and opened the door just as the chief was about to knock.

"Henry."

"Hello, Chief Ramsey."

"Mind if I come in?"

"No, not at all." Henry pushed open the screen door so the chief could enter. He walked in and looked around.

"Hi, Sarah."

"Hi, Jack." Sarah and Jack were on a first name basis. They grew up and went to school together.

After a short silence, Henry nervously asked, "Is there something wrong? Is this about Luke? He told us what happened."

"No, no. That's a fine boy you have."

"If it's about the other night, we're taking care of it. Lucas will be staying right here unless we send him on an errand. That's where he is right now. Gettin' a bag of potatoes from Ristom's grocery. He'll be back here shortly," said Sarah.

"Please don't be too hard on him. He's just a boy. Remember the things we did when we were that age?" said Chief Ramsey.

"Yeah, I remember my mother wanting to pull her hair out. Not to mention ours," said Henry. They managed a smile which helped relax the mood.

"Anyway, the reason I stopped by was to give you some information on the two prisoners I arrested the other night. They may or may not make bail. But regardless, I think they will serve some time in jail for grave robbery, and when they're released, they'll probably leave town and we will never hear from them again. I'm not telling you what to do. You may want to keep a close eye on the boys. You don't want them to be prisoners in their own homes. You know, let boys be boys. Let them enjoy their summer. Just try to—"

Henry cut him off. "After what you told us about those men, you think that would be wise?"

"If they make bail, we will be keeping an eye on them, and if they make any kind of move, I'll make sure they are put away for a long time. I'll keep you updated. Well, I won't take up any more of your time. Oh, just for your information, I'll give the Johnsons a heads-up too.

"Thanks, Chief," said Henry.

As Luke was riding up into the yard on his bike, he could see the taillights of the police car as it pulled away.

Uh-oh. This can't be good, he thought.

He brought the bag of potatoes into the kitchen and set them by the sink. When he turned to go to his bedroom, his mother was standing a couple of feet away. She grabbed him and hugged him tight.

"I love you, son," she said.

"I love you too, Mom. Are you okay?"

She nodded and swatted him on the behind and said, "Go get cleaned up. Won't take me long to fix these potatoes. Everything else is ready."

Luke walked to his room wondering what that was all about. He shrugged his shoulders and quietly said, "I guess it was best for me to tell the truth about what happened the other night.

At the dinner table, Luke's parents explained to him about the chief's visit and for him to keep his eyes open for anything unusual.

The next morning, Chief Ramsey and Officer Jones escorted the prisoners to the courthouse for their arraignment. They all sat quietly waiting for the judge. When he walked in, the bailiff called out, "All rise."

The judge sat down and uttered, "You may be seated."

The judge looked at the two defendants and proceeded, "Gentlemen, I have read the complaint against you and will ask each of you, "How do you plead?"

The two defendants looked at each other and simultaneously turned to the judge and said, "Not guilty."

The judge looked over the top of his glasses and stared at them. Realizing their shortcomings,

Freeman elbowed Toomey, and they quickly restated their answers. "Uh, not guilty, Your Honor." This appeared to have satisfied the judge, so he continued.

"I have noted your plea and will set trial for August 10, one week from today. Bail is set at $500 each. Do you have the money to post bail?"

Butch Freeman spoke up, "Yes, we do, Your Honor."

Chief Ramsey had a puzzled look on his face. He thumbed through the paperwork until he found the contents that noted what each of the defendants had on them when they were arrested. One of them had $11 and the other $17. He thought about it for a few seconds. He knew it was smart of them to plead innocent. If they would have pleaded guilty, the judge would have decided their punishment. Given their criminal history, they would have gone straight to jail. Pleading innocent gave them the option of bailing out and time to get a lawyer. They weren't fooling Jack Ramsey though. He knew if they were able to make bail, they would leave town and never be heard from again—that is, until they were arrested for another crime probably hundreds of miles away. The judge dismissed the court and exited.

Chief Ramsey turned to the two defendants and asked, "How do you plan on getting the money for bail?"

"Where's our car?" asked Freeman.

"It's in the impoundment behind the station. Why?"

"'Cause we got money in it. Ain't no law against that is there, Chief?" Freeman said sarcastically.

Not to be gotten the better of, Chief Ramsey shot back, "Nope, as long as it's not stolen money."

Still handcuffed, the chief escorted the two offenders to the impoundment area. Officer Jones retrieved the car keys from an envelope that contained the belongings of Butch Freeman and met them at their car. He started to unlock the car door when Freeman spoke up.

"No need for that. Just open the trunk."

When the trunk was opened, Freeman made a step toward the car. Chief Ramsey put his hand up in front of Freeman and said, "Stop! Tell me where the money is, and I'll get it."

"Sure, lift up the spare tire and the blanket underneath it," said Freeman.

Toomey grimaced. Apparently, he didn't even know where Freeman was keeping their money.

"Strange place to keep your money," Officer Jones said.

"Hey, you never know what's going to happen when you're on the road. Lots of crooks out there."

"You don't say," said the chief.

Chief Ramsey picked up the brown paper bag and closed the trunk. "Let's go, boys. You can count it inside." They walked back inside to the chief's office.

"Can you get their things, Martin?"

"Yes, sir. Be right back."

"Okay, I need each of you to sign a couple of forms. The bail is $500 apiece."

"Yeah, we know," said Toomey.

Officer Jones returned with two envelopes that contained Freeman's and Toomey's personal belongings that were confiscated when they were arrested. Freeman looked inside his and then looked up at Chief Ramsey. Knowing what Freeman was thinking, Chief Ramsey responded by saying, "When you produce a concealed carry permit, the gun will be returned to you." Freeman looked down and shook his head. They signed their release forms, picked up their envelopes, grabbed the brown paper bag which contained what was left of their money, and turned to walk out.

"By the way, make sure you stay in town." He knew there were three lawyers in town, but he doubted they would try to contact any of them. His gut feeling said they would be skipping town before their trial.

"Are we done here?" asked Toomey.

"For now," said the chief.

Freeman and Toomey turned and walked out.

"Martin," said Ramsey, "something tells me we're just getting started. Do me a favor and take some pictures of that bail money. We'll run the serial numbers and make sure it didn't come from a bank robbery. My hunch is that's some dirty money."

8

"Let's get something to eat," said Freeman. They drove around town until they found a small diner on the outskirts of town. It didn't look like much, but on the other hand, they weren't accustomed to eating at fancy, high-dollar restaurants.

*****

Luke walked into the house after helping his dad feed the animals. Wiping the sweat from his forehead, he asked his mom if there was any lemonade. After working outside in the heat, nothing quenched his thirst better than a tall, ice-cold glass of lemonade.

"How about you go wash up, and I'll make us a fresh pitcher."

Luke smiled and headed for the bathroom. When he walked back into the kitchen, there on the kitchen table sat a fresh pitcher of lemonade, and right beside it his glass filled right to the top. It took Luke about five seconds to empty the glass.

"Whoa! Slow down, young man. You're going to get a stomachache."

Luke just smiled and said, "Thanks, Mom." He got up from the table to go back outside when his mom said, "Hey, Luke, I need you to go to the store and get some lettuce and tomatoes for our salad tonight." Because of the drought and the tornado earlier in the summer that destroyed a big portion of their crops, they were forced to buy a lot of vegetables they would normally have on hand.

Luke rode his bike into town, and as fate would have it, right past the roadside diner where Freeman and Toomey were eating. Sitting in a booth at the front window, they had a clear view of all the traffic coming and going. Freeman raised his fork to his mouth to take a bite of steak, but it never made it. He was staring out the window at a kid passing by on a bike.

"What's wrong, Butch?" Toomey asked.

"That kid on the bike."

Toomey turned around in the booth and watched Luke stop and get off his bike at Ristom's store, about a block past the diner.

"Yeah, so, it's a kid on a bike."

"I've seen that kid before. When he comes out of the store, I want to get another look at him." After about ten minutes, Luke walked out, hopped on his bike, and headed for home. He passed directly in front of the diner. Freeman and Toomey had already finished eating and were sitting in their car so they could get a good look at him. He passed within a few feet of their car. He didn't even notice them. His mind was a thousand miles away, like it always seemed to be while riding his bike. The two men thought for a few seconds, and like a light bulb being switched on, looked at each other.

"It's that kid," said Freeman excitedly.

"From the cemetery," Toomey said.

"Not only that. He's the same kid that I ran into at that department store a couple of months ago. You know, the one that kept smiling at me."

"You think him and that other kid told the police about us? I mean why else would they have been at the cemetery with that cop?" said Toomey.

"Hmm. There's a good chance of it," said Freeman. "Let's follow him."

Luke pedaled up to Josh's house, got off his bike, and knocked on the door. He had no idea he was being followed. He was looking around while waiting for someone to answer and noticed a car passing by very slow. He could tell they were looking his way but didn't think anything about it. About that time, Josh opened the door.

"Hey, Josh, I'm on my way home from the grocery store. Wanna come over and play baseball?"

"Sure! Good timing. I just finished my chores. Hey, Mom, I'm going to Luke's to throw the ball."

"Okay, be careful."

The boys headed to Luke's house. It was only about five minutes if they pedaled hard. Just as they were pulling into Luke's yard, the same car Luke saw earlier at Josh's was coming down the street. Only this time it was moving even slower. He watched as the car drove by, still not able to make out who it was. He watched until the car was out of sight.

Hmm, must be lost, he thought.

"Come on, Luke. Let's throw the ball."

"Okay. Coming."

While the boys were outside playing, the phone rang. It was Chief Ramsey. "Hello, Sarah, it's Jack. I just wanted to let you know the two fellows we had locked up posted bail. They're out for now, awaiting trial. I'll call the Johnsons and give them a heads-up too."

"Thanks, Jack. We'll keep an eye on the boys."

"Boy it's hot out here," said Luke.

"Yeah, we need to cool off."

Luke thought for a second. "Hey, we haven't been to Logan Lake all summer. You think your mom and dad would let you go?"

"When?" asked Josh.

"I'm not sure. Let me ask my parents."

The boys ran inside the house. "Hey, Dad, you think we could go to Logan Lake?" We haven't been there all summer." Mr. Meyers rubbed his chin. He knew school was right around the corner, and they wouldn't have many more chances.

"Let me check with your mom."

They could hear his mom and dad discussing the matter. Mr. Meyers returned and said, "I tell you what, how does Saturday sound to you? I think we could all use a break. We'll drive over there, find a good spot, cook some hotdogs, and make a day of it.

"Great!" said Luke. Let's call your mom and dad and see if they will let you go."

"Okay."

Freeman and Toomey drove up and down the road in front of Luke's a few more times. The road didn't appear to be traveled very much. The more they drove and talked, the more they convinced themselves it was the boys' fault they were caught at the cemetery. Payback was imminent. They made a final pass by Luke's when Freeman stopped the car about a quarter of a mile down the road. He slowly backed the car up a few feet and stopped. He looked for a few seconds, got out of the car, and walked to the side of the road. It appeared to be a deserted old driveway that hadn't been used in years. The brush was thick, and passersby would not even notice them. He walked back to the car and got in.

"This will be perfect when the time comes," said Freeman.

He looked over at Toomey, and both men nodded.

"We better stay in town for a couple of days," said Freeman. I'm sure the police will be watching us."

"Yeah," said Toomey. "We passed a motel near that diner we ate at earlier. Didn't look too bad."

Freeman pulled the car out onto the road and headed back to town. Their plan was coming together.

Chief Ramsey was busy working at his desk. He always seemed to be overwhelmed with paperwork. Being stuck in a chair behind a desk, reading and signing documents was the last thing he felt like doing on a Friday morning. It was what he liked the least about his job, but he knew it came with the territory. It had been a busy week, and he was hoping to be finished by noon. He loved the outdoors, and the fish were biting, so he hoped to get the weekend started early.

He worked tirelessly until he came to the last of the documents. He looked it over, signed it, and closed the folder. It was now a quarter to twelve, and he was ready to go.

The chief looked up as Officer Martin was passing in the hallway.

"Hey, Martin."

"Yeah, Chief."

"I'm getting ready to leave. I'll check on Freeman and Toomey on my way home. If you don't mind, check on them tomorrow. If you don't see their car at the motel, let me know. Me and the missus will be up at the camp."

"Sure thing, Chief."

Chief Ramsey walked through the station to let everyone know where he would be for the weekend. If they needed anything, he wouldn't be far away.

He passed by the motel, and to his relief, Freeman's car was still parked in the same spot.

At least I can get the weekend started on the right foot, he thought. He smiled and drove home.

9

Friday night came, and Luke hopped into bed. He knew it would be hard to sleep tonight. He was too excited about going swimming tomorrow. After tossing and turning a while, he finally dozed off.

Saturday morning was coming to life, and Luke was up early. He made sure the animals had plenty of food and water for the day. He was ready to go, but he did make time to eat breakfast. When he finished, he went to his room and gathered his swimming trunks, a couple of towels, and an extra pair of clothes. He dug through his closet and found his frisbee, an essential while playing on the sandbar. He stuffed everything in his duffel bag and thought to himself, *Let's go*. He walked into the kitchen. Mrs. Myers was almost finished gathering food and drinks for the trip. "Where's Dad?" he asked.

"He's outside putting supplies in the car."

Luke walked outside to see if his dad could use a hand. "Hey, Dad," need some help loading the car?"

"Sure. Grab those lawn chairs on the side of the house."

Mr. Meyers shoved a rolled-up awning into the trunk. This would help shade them from the sun. Luke brought the chairs to the car and handed them to his dad. He loaded them and closed the trunk.

"That ought to do it. We better get moving if we want to get a good spot. I'm sure there's going to be plenty of people there today." Mrs. Myers put the food and goodies on the front seat. The family piled in and headed down the road to pick up Josh. When they pulled into Josh's yard, he was sitting on the front doorsteps. He hopped up, grabbed his bag, and ran to the car.

"Morning, all!" Josh said.

They all returned the greeting.

"It should take us about thirty minutes to get there if the traffic is light. We'll look for a barbecue pit and park next to it. It would be a big help if you boys would help me set up the awning before you hit the water. It should only take a few minutes."

"Sure thing, Dad."

They turned off the main road and arrived at the lake a couple of minutes later. There were already a lot of people there, but they were able to find the perfect spot, about thirty yards from the bank, with a beautiful view of the lake. They all pitched in unloading the car. When they finished, the boys headed for the water.

"We'll eat in about an hour!" Mrs. Myers shouted. Luke turned and waved in acknowledgment.

The boys walked down to the bank and looked around to see if they recognized any of their friends from school. They spotted a group of girls at one end of the sandbar and walked toward them. As they got closer, they realized Jordan Meeker was there, trying to impress the girls. Neither one of them cared much for him. He was rude and obnoxious.

"I don't know why them girls hang around him," Luke said to Josh.

"Me neither."

One of the girls in the crowd shouted, "Hey, Luke. Hey, Josh!"

Everyone turned and waved at them, and then they heard an unmistakable voice say, "Hey, losers." The kids in the crowd laughed.

Luke spoke up. "We're not losers."

"You are, if I say you are," said Jordan. Some of the girls giggled again.

One of them spoke up, "We're getting ready to play volleyball. You and Josh want to play?"

Before either of them could answer, Jordan chimed in, "Volleyball is for girls. You two should fit right in." Once again, some giggles were heard from the crowd. "I'll catch you girls later. I'm gonna get in the water. See ya, losers."

Luke and Josh looked at each other and shook their heads.

"Pay no attention to him," said a voice. "He just thinks he's Mr. Big Shot because he's the captain of the football team." It was Joley Newsome.

Luke wasn't sure what to say. "Oh, that's okay, he doesn't bother me." But she knew he wasn't being totally truthful.

"You guys sure you don't want to play volleyball?" she asked.

"Umm, probably not right now. We're going to walk down to the water. But thanks anyway," said Luke.

"Okay, but if you change your minds, you know where we'll be."

Luke and Josh walked away feeling embarrassed, but Luke wasn't one for confrontation. He knew it was better to look the other way. Besides, he knew "what goes around comes around". They walked along the bank, talking while the water covered their feet.

"Boy, that guy is a knucklehead," said Josh.

"Yeah, but some people are just like that. Guess you gotta take the bad with the good."

It was nearing noon, and their stomachs were saying it was time to eat. They heard a commotion in the water, looked, and realized it was Jordan. He was splashing two nearby swimmers.

They didn't appear to be very amused. Luke shook his head and thought, *He never stops*, then headed for the car. Mrs. Myers had lunch ready, and it couldn't have come too soon. After they finished lunch, she offered the boys some dessert. They both accepted.

"You boys may want to let that food settle for a while before you get into the water. Don't want to get cramps," said his dad. Luke didn't know if that was just an old wives' tale or not, but if his dad said it, he wasn't going to argue. They lolled around the car for a while, throwing the football. Once they worked up a good sweat, it was time to get in the water.

They walked down to the water. The area was overcrowded with swimmers.

"I guess everybody decided to swim at the same time," said Josh. They looked around and noticed there was nobody swimming on the point around the bend. Hardly anyone took the time to go out there. There wasn't much of a sandbar, and the water was deep. Unless you wanted to swim all the way over there, it was a bit of a challenge. The old path was overgrown with bushes, and fallen trees had created numerous obstacles. It took the boys about ten minutes to maneuver their way through. The payoff was worth it. The water was crystal clear.

They swam out a little way and dove down. The plant life on the bottom was undisturbed, and every once in a while, they would catch a glimpse of fish darting about as if they were playing tag. This was the life. Almost paradise. They surfaced, swam back to shore, and rested a few minutes. As they were getting ready to take another swim, Luke noticed someone floating on an inner tube. He watched for a few seconds and realized it was Jordan Meeker. He had drifted about halfway between Luke and Josh and the other swimmers at the main sandbar. *He must be showing off for someone*, thought Luke. He rolled his eyes and dove back into the water.

When Luke surfaced, he looked around and noticed the inner tube but no Jordan. *Hmm*, he thought. He treaded water for a while, watching for any sign of Jordan. Then he saw some movement in the water about thirty yards away. A hand came up as if it were reaching for the sky. Jordan's head surfaced for a second, gasping for air, then retreated back under the water. Luke realized he wasn't playing. He was in trouble.

Luke had attended a lifeguard camp the prior summer. He had learned that despite what people thought, when a person was drowning, they hardly made a sound at all. He started swimming toward Jordan. He hadn't surfaced again, and Luke knew time was critical. When he reached the area where he had last seen Jordan, he dove down. He spotted him in the near distance. Luke knew when someone was struggling underwater, they were scared and would grab for anything they could get their hands on. Luke was trained to come up behind the person and slide your arm up underneath theirs. This would allow you a free arm to propel both of you to the surface. When they reached the top of the water, Luke lay back to allow Jordan's head to stay above the water.

"I-I can't swim." Jordan was coughing and flailing his arms about, but Luke was able to hold onto him and get him to the inner tube. About that time, Josh arrived and grabbed one of Jordan's forearms and put it on top of the inner tube. After a couple of minutes, Jordan stopped coughing and spitting up water, but he was completely worn out from the fight.

All the commotion had caught the attention of some of the swimmers. When Jordan regained his composure and was able to talk, he said, "Thanks. I would have drowned if it weren't for you. This is so embarrassing."

They paddled with their feet until they were able to touch bottom near the sandbar. Some of the onlookers had gathered and were watching them. One of the girls shouted out, "Hey, what happened out there?"

The three boys looked at each other. Jordan's shoulders slumped, knowing what Luke and Josh were going to say. But to his amazement, Luke spoke up and said, "Aw nothing, we were just horsin' around out there. Jordan was laughing, and he swallowed some water. We're all okay."

Jordan and Luke looked at each other, and Jordan mouthed, "Thanks."

Luke nodded and said, "You're welcome."

Changing the subject, Luke said, "Hey, my mom made some brownies. You want one?"

Jordan smiled and said, "You bet." After eating their desserts, the boys threw the frisbee for a while and even played volleyball with the girls, including Jordan. At the end of the day, they all said their goodbyes.

Jordan walked up to Luke and Josh and said, "I'm sorry I've been such a jerk to you guys. I'm probably the last person you'd want to help."

Josh felt like saying "You darn right," but Jordan sounded sincere.

"Thanks again, and I truly am sorry. I'll see you guys at school." They all smiled then turned and went their separate ways. The Myers loaded everything up in the car and headed home.

"You boys had a full day. I'm sure you're worn out," said Mr. Myers.

"Yes, sir," said Luke.

The boys were quiet the rest of the way home. They were tired but had the satisfaction of knowing they had not only saved someone's life but had secured a new friendship. They had no trouble sleeping that night.

10

L uke was an early riser on Sunday mornings. He knew the animals had to be fed and watered before church. After church, the Myers ate lunch, then Henry settled into his favorite chair to watch a baseball game on television. Mrs. Meyers decided to work on some sewing she had been putting off for days.

"You have any plans, Luke?" she asked.

"Mmm, I thought maybe I would go outside and oil the chain on my bike. Other than that, nothing really."

"When you finish, do you mind running to the grocery store with your dad? I'm making steak and gravy tonight, and we're getting low on rice."

"Okay, but I can ride my bike. It won't take me long."

"I'd rather you go with your dad for now. It's a long ride to the grocery store, and until those men are put away or leave town, I would feel better if you don't ride your bike that far."

"I understand, Mom. Hey, would it be okay if Josh came over and ate supper with us? Maybe we can play some ball before we eat."

"I don't see why not."

"Thanks."

Luke went outside and oiled the chain on his bike. He looked his bike over and realized it was about time for a new one. He'd had this one for over two years and was outgrowing it.

Hmm, that'll be a good present for my birthday, he thought.

"What are you thinking about, son?" Luke didn't realize his dad had walked outside and was standing beside him.

"Huh, oh, just thinking about what I want for my next birthday."

"You ready to go?"

Luke and his dad arrived at the grocery store. Luke hopped out and went inside. He picked up a large bag of rice, paid for it, and went back to the car.

"Hey, Dad, can we stop at Josh's? Mom said he could come over and eat supper."

When they pulled up in Josh's yard, Luke rolled down the window and shouted, "Josh!"

Josh was walking toward the house from the barn.

"Hey, long time no see," said Josh.

"I just saw you yesterday," Luke said.

"I know. I heard that on a TV show," laughed Josh.

"Oh, okay. Well, anyway, you want to come eat supper and throw the football?" asked Luke.

"Is it okay with your dad?"

"Sure."

"Okay, let me check."

Josh returned with his mom. "Hey, Luke. Hey, Henry. You sure it's okay for Josh to go eat supper?"

"Yes, ma'am," said Luke.

"He's welcome anytime, Alice," said Henry.

"Did you finish your chores, Josh?"

Josh thought for a second, looked at Luke and said, "I'll meet you at your house. I have to pick up my room, and then I'll be over. It won't take but a few minutes, so I'll just ride my bike."

The boys played catch with the football, baseball, and tossed the frisbee until they started getting hungry. They walked inside to see if supper was ready. "By the time you boys get washed up, I'll have everything on the table," said Mrs. Myers.

11

Their trial was only two days away, but Freeman and Toomey had no plans to be there. They planned to tie up a couple of loose ends and then disappear. It was getting late, so they decided to make a pass by Luke's house. By the time they reached Luke's, it was nearly dark. They could barely make out the two bicycles laying on their sides near the front door.

"Well, looky here," said Freeman. "Looks like there's two kids at the house. Doubt if they'll be getting back out this late. Things are looking up."

They passed the house and found their hiding spot. He backed the car in until it was not visible from the road.

"We'll sleep here tonight. In the morning, we'll keep an eye out for them," said Freeman.

Toomey shook his head in agreement.

As they finished dinner, Josh knew it was getting late, so he'd better get home.

"You boys get enough to eat?"

"Yes, ma'am," they both said.

"For the life of me, I don't know where you two put all that food, but as long as you'll keep eating, I'll keep cooking."

"Hey, Josh, you want to spend the night?"

"Hmm, I don't know if my mom will let me."

"Hang on. Hey, Mom, since it's getting so late, would it be alright if Josh spends the night?"

"Sure, I don't mind."

"Would you mind calling his mom and see if it's okay?" asked Luke.

"Yes, give me just a minute."

The boys hustled into Luke's bedroom but kept one ear open for the *okay* for the sleepover.

"Hi, Alice. This is Sarah. Sure, they're alright. Sorry, supper was later than usual tonight, and since it's already dark, you mind Josh staying the night?" Sarah listened to Alice's reply and said, "Yes, I agree. I don't want him on the road this late by himself either."

"Uh-huh, I'm sure Luke would like that," said Sarah. "Okay, I'll send the boys over in the morning."

Mrs. Meyers stopped at Luke's room, tapped on the door, and pushed it open.

"Mrs. Johnson said it would be okay if Josh spent the night. She said for you two to go eat breakfast at their house in the morning. She'll fix enough food for an army," Mrs. Meyers said grinning.

"Good night, boys."

"Night, Mom."

"Good night, Mrs. Meyers."

About an hour later, Sarah and Henry turned in for the night. Luke and Josh spent the next two hours talking about cars they liked, their favorite sports teams, and of course, girls. Soon they were fast asleep.

It didn't take long for a new day to dawn. The sun was rising, the animals were stirring, and the Meyers were sitting down to eat breakfast.

*****

Chief Ramsey walked into his office early, knowing this was going to be a busy week. He grabbed his cup and headed down the hallway to fill it with some fresh coffee while greeting everyone along the way. Officer Martin was waiting for him and handed him a folder.

"This came in late Friday afternoon after you had already left. I hated to bother you so I thought it could wait until today."

He opened the folder. Across the top it read: Attention Chief Ramsey. He read the contents and closed the folder.

"Well, Martin, this just keeps getting better and better. It appears the bail money Freeman and Toomey used was stolen. I'm going to see if they're still at the motel. If they are, I'll let you know. You and a couple of officers can meet me there, and we'll arrest them and put them back where they belong."

He had a bad feeling about Freeman and Toomey. Call it a hunch, but his instinct had served him well in the past. He drove past the motel, but the car was gone. *They could be anywhere*, he thought. He decided to make a pass by the Johnsons' and Meyers'.

12

"Wake up!" said Freeman. "You're slobberin' all over yourself."

"Huh, what?" said Toomey. He wiped his mouth, then wiped his hand on his pants.

Freeman started the car and eased onto the main road. He looked both ways, then turned the car in the direction of the Meyers' house. When the house was in sight, he pulled over on the side of the road.

The bikes were still laying in the same spots as they were the night before.

"We'll sit here for a little while," said Freeman.

"Yeah, I doubt if those boys will stay cooped up inside the house all day," Toomey said.

Freeman nodded and grunted.

Mrs. Meyers walked to the door of Luke's bedroom and shouted, "You boys going to get up? Daylight's burning. You don't want to miss out on breakfast." She knew that would get their attention.

"Sure. Thanks, Mom."

Luke and Josh rolled out of bed, yawned, stretched, and put their clothes on. They walked into the kitchen. Mr. Meyers was sitting at the table reading the newspaper, his daily ritual. He looked up over the paper and said, "Morning, boys." Before they could return the greeting, Mrs. Meyers chimed in, "You boys better get moving! I'm sure Mrs. Johnson has breakfast on the table. Oh, by the way, rain's moving in, so be careful. Lucas, call me when you boys get to Josh's, and call me when you get ready to come home so I can watch for you."

"Yes, ma'am."

The boys went outside and hopped on their bikes. They could see the dark clouds in the distance.

"We better pedal fast before we get wet," said Josh.

"Bingo," said Freeman.

He started the car and put it in gear.

The boys looked both ways as they reached the main road, then turned left and headed for Josh's. Luke noticed the car sitting on the side of the road to the right.

It looks familiar, he thought.

Could that be the same car that kept passing by the other day? He looked over his shoulder and noticed the car was now driving on the road. He had a bad feeling, then his eyes widened. *Could it be*?

It was starting to rain. Luke looked over his shoulder again. The car was gaining on them.

"Josh, I'm not sure, but I think we've got company."

"Wh-who?"

"I think it's the guys from the cemetery."

"Wh-what?" Josh looked back in disbelief.

The boys were pedaling as hard as they could, but the car was gaining fast. They were approaching a curve in the road. A bridge connected the road over a steep gully and a small creek. The car was close enough they could hear the engine. The rain was falling steady now, causing the road to puddle with water. The bumper of the car was now within a few feet of the bicycles. The boys knew what the driver's intent was.

Freeman punched the accelerator. Luke and Josh heard the engine rev. The rear tires temporarily lost traction on the wet road, causing the rear end of the car to skid sideways. This was the break the boys needed. Freeman quickly gained control of the car.

Knowing there was no time and nowhere else to go, Luke and Josh looked at each other and knew what they had to do. They turned the front tires of their bikes slightly to the right and bailed off the side of the road, down the ravine. The angle was too steep. Their bikes tumbled end over end until they came to a stop where the ground leveled out.

Freeman was going too fast and could not make the curve. He lost control of the car. It crashed through the bridge railing, down the ravine, and landed in the creek.

Chief Ramsey was driving from the opposite direction and saw the whole event unfold. He could hardly believe what was happening. It looked like a scene out of a movie. He grabbed his radio and called dispatch.

"Helen!"

"Go ahead, Jack." She could hear the urgency in his voice.

"I need an ambulance and backup on FM844 at Red Hawk Creek bridge."

"10-4, will do."

The chief's car skidded to a stop on top of the bridge. He jumped out and looked over the edge. The car was sitting in the water, badly distorted, with smoke coming out from under the front end. He panned the area for the boys and spotted them near the bottom of the ravine, in a patch of weeds. He cupped his hands around his mouth and yelled, "Are you boys alright?"

Josh was in a sitting position looking at his body. He was moving his arms and legs to make sure everything worked. A few scratches, a tear in his jeans, but miraculously, nothing else. He was okay.

"I think so," Josh hollered.

"Just stay put. We'll have somebody here soon to get you."

Josh looked over at Luke who was struggling to push himself up. He caught a glimpse of Luke's left arm. "Luke don't try to get up. Let me see. Yeah, your arm's broken."

Luke looked down at the contorted arm. "Aw man," he said in disgust.

"Lay back down. Let me check your other arm and your legs."

Luke moved his right arm and legs. They all seemed to be in working condition.

Josh yelled up to the chief, "Luke's arm is broken."

Chief gave him a motion of acknowledgment.

About five minutes later, two ambulances and two other officers arrived. Two minutes later, the Meyers and Johnsons were on the scene. Helen, the dispatcher, had notified the parents that the boys had been in an accident but were okay. This was little comfort to either of them.

The paramedics quickly retrieved their equipment. One of them donned a harness while the other connected him to a rope. The chief pointed to where the boys were located. The medic slowly rappelled the steep embankment until he reached the boys. He positioned Luke's arm in a sling, connected him around the waist, and motioned to his attendant on the side of the road. Mr. Johnson joined in and helped pull the rope until Luke and the medic were up on the road.

The Meyers could hardly contain themselves. They ran to Luke and held him tight as tears streamed down Mrs. Meyers's face. They sat down on the rear bumper of the ambulance.

"Oh, Luke, I'm so sorry. We should have watched you closer than we did."

"I'm okay, Mom and don't worry, you watch me close enough!" Luke gave her a smile. She grinned and hugged him tighter.

The medic returned to Josh and secured him. Once they were safely on the road, the medic's attention turned to the mangled car in the creek.

A doctor and nurse on the scene tended to the boys. They bandaged the scrapes on Josh and checked his vital signs.

"Josh, you're going to be fine," said Dr. Ross. He turned to Josh's parents and said, "Have him take it easy for a couple of days, and he'll be back to normal in no time."

Dr. Ross looked at Luke and said, "Now you, young man, are going to need a cast on that arm. Other than that, I think you'll be all right too. A few bumps and bruises, but they'll heal. Sarah, bring him by the office in about an hour."

Mr. Meyers had walked off to talk to Chief Ramsey. When he returned, he looked at them both and said, "Chief Ramsey said we could go home. There's no need for us to hang around here. They have a crew at the car checking on the men inside. He said he would give us an update later."

They walked back to their car. Luke looked over his shoulder toward Josh and said, "Hey, Josh, I'll call you later." Josh shook his head to acknowledge, and then the boys got into their cars and headed home.

"Mom," said Luke.

"Yes, dear?"

"Is there anything to eat? We missed breakfast, and I'm starving."

Henry and Sarah looked at each other and smiled.

"I don't think there's anything that will stop that boy from eating," said his dad.

"Sure, hon. I'll fix you whatever you want. I think you've earned it!"

After eating, Luke and his parents drove to the doctor's office. The pain in his arm was getting worse, and Luke wasn't looking forward to what the doctor was going to do to it. He knew it would get worse before it got better. It didn't take long, and the doctor walked in.

"Okay, let's take some X-rays so we can get a better look at that arm."

Afterward, the doctor excused himself, and fifteen minutes later, returned with the pictures and a smile on his face.

"Good news, Luke. It was a clean break. It's still pretty well-lined-up. I'll make a small adjustment, put a cast on it, and give you a prescription for pain. You'll be out of here in no time. Oh, and one more thing, no more daredevil bicycle stunts for a while, okay?" They both laughed.

"Yes, sir, I promise!"

After a short trip home, Luke went to his bedroom and lay down. He was ready for some quiet time. He listened to the radio until his mom called him to supper. There wasn't much conversation, and after he ate, he told his parents he was tired and was going to bed. They didn't question him. After the day he'd had, it was understandable.

Luke lay in bed staring at the ceiling, listening to the crickets chirping outside. Then it hit him. He was overwhelmed by the day's events and how things could have turned out. Tears filled his eyes and ran down his cheeks onto his pillow. He had a good long cry. Something that he needed to do. When he was done, he closed his eyes and went to sleep.

When he woke the next morning, he could hear a conversation of familiar voices. He walked into the living room. The chief was there talking to his parents. They looked his direction and his dad said, "Morning, son."

Chief Ramsey spoke up. "Hey, Luke, it's good to hear that you and Josh are going to be all right. Them other two fellows weren't so lucky. They're going to be in the hospital for a while. They have some serious injuries, but they'll recover. Then they're going away for a long, long time. You won't ever have to worry about them again. Well, I better get moving. I have a lot of work to do."

"Thanks, Chief," said Henry and Sarah.

Luke walked to the window and watched the chief back out of the yard. He followed the car with his eyes until it was out of sight. He stood there and thought to himself, *This is the strangest summer I can ever remember*, then walked back to his bedroom.

13

This was the last week of summer break, and it was passing quickly. The weekend before school started was approaching. Luke was in his bedroom looking over his class schedule when there was a knock at the front door. Mrs. Meyers answered the door. It was a young girl, about Luke's age, and she was holding an envelope.

"May I help you?"

The girl nervously replied, "Yes, ma'am. My name is Joley Newsome. I go to school with Luke. Is he here?"

"Yes, please come in. Luke!" she called. "You have a visitor."

Mrs. Meyers hurried back to the kitchen where Henry was drinking a cup of coffee.

"It's a girl! For Luke!" she said excitedly.

"Yes, I heard."

Luke walked into the living room. You could have heard a pin drop. His face told the whole story. *Why on earth is the prettiest girl in school standing in our living room?* he thought.

"Hi, Luke," said Joley, noticing the blank look on his face. "Are you okay?"

"Huh? Oh yeah, sure. I just wasn't… Uh, never mind."

"I heard you were a hero! Helping the chief catch those bad guys."

"A hero? Where did you hear that?"

"Oh, I don't know. Word travels fast in this town."

"I'm not sure about being a hero. Josh and I darn near got ourselves killed."

"What?" said Joley, sounding startled.

"Oh, don't worry. This broken arm appears to be the worst of it."

"I'm glad you and Josh are okay. I better be going. My mom is waiting for me in the car." She turned to leave and remembered. "Oh, Luke, I almost forgot. The reason I stopped by was to give you this." She handed him an envelope.

"I'm having a back-to-school party Friday night. Nothing special, just a few friends. There'll be music and plenty to eat. Oh, and tell Josh to come too. Maybe you and he can fill us in on what happened the other day. I hope you'll come!"

"Sure, I'll be there."

Luke stood at the front door and watched Joley get into the car. She waved. Luke waved and shut the door. He walked back to his bedroom and lay across the bed. He opened the envelope and read the invitation. It gave the date, time, and address of the party, but there was one added note at the bottom that read: "Hey Luke, I hope you come to the party. I would really like to get to know you better. Joley."

Luke sat up on the bed. A big smile came over his face, and he thought, *This has got to be the best start of a school year that I can ever remember!*

ABOUT THE AUTHOR

Mike Doyle was raised in the small southeast Texas city of Nederland. Growing up near a wildlife marsh, he and his friends embarked on many adventures and campouts. They often filled the nights telling stories while lying underneath the stars. It was not unusual to cross the paths of alligators, snakes, rabbits, nutria rats, ducks, or geese while trudging through the marsh. He enjoyed the beauty that Mother Nature had to offer and would spend hours watching many of the animals in their natural habitat. Mike hopes this book will instill the values of honesty, good manners, and friendship, as well as encourage others to get out and embrace adventures of their own.

At nineteen, he met Cindy, his wife-to-be. They raised two daughters, Brandi and Brooke. Mike began writing short stories and poems dealing with some of his own personal experiences. Two of his poems,

"Cindy, My Marquis" and "When Night Comes," have been published in *The Promise of Dawn, The National Library of Poetry* and *Poetry's Elite: The Best Poets of 2000* respectively. Watching his grandchildren, Gavin, Nathan, Kieran, and Madison, growing up has inspired him to continue writing.

CPSIA information can be obtained
at www.ICGtesting.com
Printed in the USA
BVHW030820180222
629290BV00004B/52

9 781649 525154